lexile 590

rl 3.8

Did he really see a ghost?

The Browns were sitting in the living room after dinner when Otto Beck burst into the house.

He opened his mouth to speak but couldn't utter a word.

"Otto, what is it?" exclaimed Mrs. Brown. "What's frightened you?"

"I—I saw *h-her!*" gasped Otto.

"Who?" asked Chief Brown.

Otto tried to tell. But the name stuck in a fresh chattering of teeth. Instead he said, "I ran all the way from Heartbreak Cove."

"But that's seven miles," Encyclopedia protested. "Your feet must be killing you."

"My feet never touched the ground," said Otto.

After a while he recovered his strength. He blinked twice and said, "I saw Jennifer MacIntosh!"

Encyclopedia gave a start.

Jennifer MacIntosh had lived in Idaville a hundred years ago.

Read all the books in the Encyclopedia Brown series!

No. 1 Encyclopedia Brown Boy Detective

*No. 2 Encyclopedia Brown and the
Case of the Secret Pitch*

No. 3 Encyclopedia Brown Finds the Clues

No. 4 Encyclopedia Brown Gets His Man

No. 5 Encyclopedia Brown Solves Them All

No. 6 Encyclopedia Brown Keeps the Peace

No. 7 Encyclopedia Brown Saves the Day

No. 8 Encyclopedia Brown Tracks Them Down

No. 9 Encyclopedia Brown Shows the Way

No. 10 Encyclopedia Brown Takes the Case

No. 11 Encyclopedia Brown Lends a Hand

*No. 12 Encyclopedia Brown and the
Case of the Dead Eagles*

*No. 13 Encyclopedia Brown and the
Case of the Midnight Visitor*

Encyclopedia Brown

No. 9

Brown

Shows the Way

By DONALD J. SOBOL

illustrated by Leonard Shortall

PUFFIN BOOKS

For Gwen and Bill Hallstrom and
Ann and Will, too

PUFFIN BOOKS
Published by the Penguin Group
Penguin Young Readers Group, 345 Hudson Street, New York, New York 10014, U.S.A.
Penguin Group (Canada), 90 Eglinton Avenue East, Suite 700,
Toronto, Ontario, Canada M4P 2Y3 (a division of Pearson Penguin Canada Inc.)
Penguin Books Ltd, 80 Strand, London WC2R 0RL, England
Penguin Ireland, 25 St Stephen's Green, Dublin 2, Ireland (a division of Penguin Books Ltd)
Penguin Group (Australia), 250 Camberwell Road, Camberwell, Victoria 3124, Australia
(a division of Pearson Australia Group Pty Ltd)
Penguin Books India Pvt Ltd, 11 Community Centre,
Panchsheel Park, New Delhi - 110 017, India
Penguin Group (NZ), 67 Apollo Drive, Rosedale, North Shore 0632, New Zealand
(a division of Pearson New Zealand Ltd)
Penguin Books (South Africa) (Pty) Ltd, 24 Sturdee Avenue,
Rosebank, Johannesburg 2196, South Africa

Registered Offices: Penguin Books Ltd, 80 Strand, London WC2R 0RL, England

First published in the United States of America by Dutton Children's Books,
a division of Penguin Young Readers Group, 1972
Published by Puffin Books, a division of Penguin Young Readers Group, 2008

11 13 15 17 19 20 18 16 14 12

THE LIBRARY OF CONGRESS HAS CATALOGED
THE DUTTON CHILDREN'S BOOKS EDITION AS FOLLOWS:
Sobol, Donald J.
Encyclopedia Brown shows the way.
(His Encyclopedia Brown book no. 9)
Summary: Encyclopedia Brown, brilliant fifth-grade amateur detective, solves ten crimes.
The reader may match solutions with those at the end of the book.
ISBN: 0-525-67216-8 (hc)
[1. Detective stories] 1. Shortall, Leonard W., illus. II. Title.
PZ7.S68524Eru [Fic] 72-2911

Puffin Books ISBN 978-0-14-241086-8

Printed in the United States of America

Contents

1. *The Case of the Growling Dog*   7

2. *The Case of the Red Harmonica*   16

3. *The Case of the Knockout Artist*   24

4. *The Case of the Headless Runner*   32

5. *The Case of the Reward Money*   40

6. *The Case of the Tooth Puller*   48

7. *The Case of the Girl Shortstop*   56

8. *The Case of the Rattlesnake's Rattle*   64

9. *The Case of the World Traveler*   71

10. *The Case of the Lady Ghost*   79

     Solutions   87

The Case of the Growling Dog

Crime was increasing everywhere in the United States. Except in Idaville.

No one—child or grown-up—got away with breaking the law in Idaville.

Apart from catching crooks lickety-quick, Idaville was like most seaside towns its size. It had rich families and poor families, lovely beaches, three movie theaters, and two delicatessens. It had churches, a synagogue, and a Little League.

And it had ten-year-old Encyclopedia Brown, America's Sherlock Holmes in sneakers.

Encyclopedia's father was chief of police. People across the country thought he was the smartest police chief on earth.

Chief Brown was smart. His officers were brave. But once in a while they came up against a crime they could not solve.

Then Chief Brown knew what to do. He went home.

Over dinner, he told Encyclopedia about the case. If Encyclopedia didn't solve the mystery before he finished his first glass of milk, his mother was disappointed. He was an only child.

Chief Brown would have liked to see a statue of Encyclopedia placed outside the FBI building. He hated keeping his son's detective work a secret.

But what good would it do to tell?

Who would believe that the mastermind behind Idaville's wonderful police record could live happily on bubble gum and popcorn? So Chief Brown said nothing.

Encyclopedia never breathed a word about the help he gave his father. He didn't want to seem different from other fifth-graders.

But he was stuck with his nickname.

Only his parents and his teachers called him by his real name, Leroy. Everyone else called him Encyclopedia.

An encyclopedia is a book or set of books filled with facts from A to Z. So was Encyclopedia's head. He was really more like an entire library, only better! His pals could ask him questions without having to whisper.

One evening over soup, Chief Brown said, "I think I know who stole Mr. Dale's electric drill last night."

"Who?" asked Mrs. Brown.

"Ed Baker," answered Chief Brown.

"Isn't he the teen-ager who stole a car in January and wrecked it over in Glenn City?" asked Encyclopedia.

Chief Brown nodded. "Ed was seen running near Mr. Dale's house last night around the time someone broke into the garage and stole the electric drill and some other tools."

"Did you arrest him, dear?" asked Mrs. Brown.

"I can't prove he did it," said Chief Brown. "Ed claims he was running to get in shape for football. He says he ran by Mr. Dale's house, but didn't stop."

"Don't you have any clues?" asked Encyclopedia.

"Two," replied Chief Brown. "We found one perfect footprint in the back yard. A left sneaker print. It was made in a spot of soft earth."

"Does it match Ed's sneaker?" asked Mrs. Brown.

"It's a half size too small," said Chief Brown heavily.

"Perhaps Mr. Dale made the print himself," suggested Mrs. Brown.

"Mr. Dale insists that no one has been in the back yard for nearly a week," said Chief Brown. "The rain yesterday afternoon washed out all the old footprints."

"So the sneaker print is new," said Encyclopedia. "It has to be the thief's. What's the second clue, Dad?"

"A piece of a shirt," said Chief Brown. "It got caught on a branch six inches above the ground."

"Did you find a torn shirt at Ed's house?" inquired Mrs. Brown.

"No," said Chief Brown. "Ed probably didn't realize he had left a footprint. But he would have discovered the rip and thrown the shirt away."

Chief Brown took a spoonful of soup. Then he continued.

"Ed must have been crawling on his stomach in order not to be seen," he said.

"What makes you think that?" asked Mrs. Brown.

"If Ed had been walking, the low branch would have ripped the bottom of his trousers, not his shirt," said Chief Brown. "But what he did next is the puzzler."

"How come?" said Encyclopedia.

"But the question is, how did he get past Rover?"

"The low branch is outside the fence that goes around Mr. Dale's house and garage," said Chief Brown. "At night, a big German shepherd named Rover runs loose inside the fence."

"Hmmm," said Encyclopedia. "Ed crawled to the fence so as not to be seen and climbed over. But the question is, how did he get past Rover?"

"Is Rover such a good watchdog?" asked Mrs. Brown.

"Rover is an attack dog," said Chief Brown. "He's trained to bark at strangers and to seize their sleeves or trousers in his teeth."

"Ed could have fed him something to keep him quiet," said Mrs. Brown.

"Rover won't take food from anyone except Mr. Dale," replied Chief Brown.

"Didn't Mr. Dale hear anything at all last night?" asked Encyclopedia.

"He heard Rover growling," said Chief Brown. "Since Rover is trained to *bark* at strangers, Mr. Dale thought the dog was chasing a frog or a rabbit. He didn't get out of bed to look."

"Perhaps Ed clubbed Rover and knocked him out," offered Mrs. Brown.

"Rover wasn't hurt," said Chief Brown. "Well . . . not in the usual way."

"What do you mean, Dad?" inquired Encyclopedia.

"This morning Mr. Dale found Rover curled up by the back door, whimpering," said Chief Brown. "The poor dog has been that way ever since. He won't eat. It's as if he had a nervous breakdown last night."

"My word!" exclaimed Mrs. Brown. She looked at Encyclopedia for help.

The boy detective had already closed his eyes. He always closed his eyes when he did his deepest thinking on a case.

Suddenly he opened them. "Ed made the footprint. He stole Mr. Dale's tools."

"But the footprint is too small," protested Mrs. Brown.

"The footprint was made when the earth was still wet from the rain," said Encyclopedia. "It's been hot and dry since."

"Of course!" cried Chief Brown. "How stupid of me! When earth dries, it shrinks. So the footprint is smaller than when it was made!"

"Oh, Leroy!" said Mrs. Brown proudly. Then she gave a troubled frown. "But how did Ed get past Rover?"

"The clue of the torn shirt tells us how, Mom," answered Encyclopedia.

HOW?

(Turn to page 87 for the solution to The Case of the Growling Dog.)

The Case of the Red Harmonica

During the winter, Encyclopedia did his detective work at the dinner table. When school let out for the summer, he decided to help the children of the neighborhood.

So he opened an office in the garage.

Every morning after breakfast he hung out his sign.

BROWN DETECTIVE AGENCY
13 Rover Avenue
Leroy Brown, President
No case too small
25¢ per day
plus expenses

Thursday afternoon a small boy entered the detective agency. He looked as happy as a cheerleader in a graveyard.

"I want to hire you," he said, putting twenty-five cents on the gasoline can beside Encyclopedia. "My name is Northcliff Hicks. Yesterday was one sad day for me."

"How come?" asked Encyclopedia.

"Soft music," replied Northcliff. "Do you know anything about soft music?"

"It goes with soft lights," answered Encyclopedia. "Is this some affair of the heart?"

"No, of the ears," said Northcliff.

He explained. Yesterday afternoon he had been sitting by Mill Pond playing his new red harmonica. A big kid had come up holding a funny whistle.

"The big kid said I might be good at playing loud," said Northcliff. "But he was better at playing soft. In fact, he claimed to be the champion soft-music player of the world."

"Could he prove it?" asked Encyclopedia.

"He challenged me to a soft-music contest," said Northcliff. "His rules."

"That really tied your lips, eh?"

"And how," said Northcliff. "Each of us had to play a tune so softly the other couldn't hear it, and yet loud enough to wake a bulldog that was sleeping across the pond."

"What did you play?"

" 'Kitten on the Keys,' " said Northcliff. "I figured a dog would go for it. I might as well have played 'The Dance of the Spanish Onion' on a frankfurter roll. That mutt lay like a dead battery. Then the big kid said he'd blow 'Coney Island Babe' on his whistle. I didn't hear a thing. But that bulldog jumped up and raced around, crazy as a bee in a honey pot."

"Don't take it so hard," said Encyclopedia. "You lost to a champion."

"I don't mind losing," said Northcliff. "But the big kid took my red harmonica. He said if *he'd* lost, he'd have given me his whistle. The liar!"

"You should have made tracks," said Encyclopedia.

"I tried, but his three friends caught me," said Northcliff. "They wore shirts with the word 'Tigers' written across the chest."

"Tigers? I should have guessed!" exclaimed Encyclopedia. "The big kid was Bugs Meany!"

Bugs Meany was the leader of a gang of tough older boys. They called themselves the Tigers. They should have called themselves the Umbrella Carts. They were always pulling something shady.

"Bugs must have blown a dog whistle," said Encyclopedia. "People can't hear it. Only dogs can."

"And I thought I was going deaf!" yelped Northcliff. "That no-good cheat! Can you get back my harmonica?"

"I can try," said Encyclopedia. "I've dealt with Bugs before. Let's go see him."

The Tigers' clubhouse was an unused tool

shed behind Mr. Sweeny's Auto Body Shop. Bugs was alone when Encyclopedia and Northcliff arrived. He was puffing "Tiger Rag" on a shiny red harmonica.

At the sight of the two boys, he switched to "Shoo, Fly, Don't Bother Me."

"Scram," he growled at Encyclopedia. "Or I'll put your head in a cast."

Encyclopedia calmly relieved Bugs of the harmonica and played "I've Heard That Song Before." Then he said, "This is Northcliff Hicks. He claims you stole his red harmonica."

"That soft-music contest was a phony," put in Northcliff. "You blew a dog whistle." He took the harmonica and rendered the opening bars of "You Took Advantage of Me."

"Soft music? Dog whistle?" cried Bugs. "You're completely out of your tree!" He snatched the harmonica and began playing "Imagination."

"You couldn't beat me in a fair contest, and you know it," said Northcliff, seizing the har-

Bugs was puffing "Tiger Rag" on a shiny red harmonica.

monica. He blew "Little White Lies."

"Oh, yeah?" said Bugs. "Let's see how well you play with loose teeth." He grabbed the harmonica and blew "Just Before the Battle, Mother."

"Cut the tough-guy stuff, Bugs," warned Encyclopedia. "That's Northcliff's harmonica. I suppose you're going to say that you found it."

Bugs blinked. "Why, so I did," he said with a sly smile. "I found it last night on a trash pile."

"Where?" demanded Northcliff.

"Along Miller Road," said Bugs. "It was dark except for some blue lights strung on the palm trees by the trash pile. I saw something red shining. I walked closer. It was the harmonica."

"That's our trash pile," Northcliff whispered to Encyclopedia. "Dad strung blue lights for a party in the back yard yesterday. But I didn't throw the harmonica away. Honest!"

Bugs grinned, raised the harmonica to his

lips, and blew "The Best Things in Life Are Free."

"Blow till you're blue in the face," said Encyclopedia. "You won't make me see red. You stole the harmonica!"

WHAT MADE
ENCYCLOPEDIA SO SURE?

(Turn to page 88 for the solution to The Case of the Red Harmonica.)

The Case of the Knockout Artist

Bugs Meany's heart burned with a great desire. It was to get even with Encyclopedia.

Bugs hated being outsmarted by the boy detective. He longed to punch Encyclopedia so hard on the jaw that the lump would come out the top of his head.

Bugs never raised a fist, though. Whenever he felt like it, he remembered Sally Kimball.

Sally was the prettiest girl in the fifth grade—and the best fighter. She had done what no boy under twelve had dreamed was possible. She had flattened Bugs Meany!

When Sally became the boy detective's junior partner, Bugs quit trying to use muscle on Ency-

24

clopedia. But he never stopped planning his day of revenge.

"Bugs hates you more than he does me," warned Encyclopedia. "He'll never forgive you for whipping him."

Just then Ike Cassidy walked into the detective agency. Ike was one of Bugs's pals.

"I'm quitting the Tigers," he announced. "I want to hire you. But you'll have to take the quarter from my pocket. I can't move my fingers."

"What's this all about?" asked Encyclopedia.

"Bugs's cousin, Bearcat Meany, is spending the weekend with him," said Ike. "Bearcat is only ten, but he's built like a caveman. Bugs said he'd give me two dollars to box a few rounds with Bearcat.

"Bearcat tripped you and stepped on your fingers?" guessed Encyclopedia.

"No, he used his head," said Ike. "I gave him my famous one-two: a left to the nose followed by a right to the chin. I must have broken both my hands hitting him."

"You should have worn boxing gloves," said Sally.

"We wore gloves," said Ike. "Man, that Bearcat is something else!"

"Did he knock you out?" asked Encyclopedia.

"He did and he didn't," said Ike. "His first punch didn't knock me out and it didn't knock me down. But it hurt so much I just had to go down anyway."

"Good grief!" gasped Encyclopedia. "H-he licked you with one punch?"

"With two," corrected Ike. "When I got up, he hit me again. I was paralyzed. I couldn't move. I couldn't move enough to fall down."

"Bearcat sounds like a coming champ," observed Sally.

"He's training for the next Olympics," said Ike.

"Isn't he a little young?" said Sally.

"You tell him that," said Ike. "He hurt me when he breathed on me."

The more Encyclopedia heard about Bearcat, the unhappier he became. "Why do you need a detective?" he asked.

"Bugs said I didn't last long enough to earn the two dollars," replied Ike. "I want you to get my money."

Encyclopedia gulped. The case looked like a bloody nose for sure. "Forget the two dollars," he suggested.

"It's a matter of pride," said Ike. "Bearcat made me mad. He said I fought like a *girl*."

"Oh, he did, did he?" cried Sally. She stamped her foot. "We'll take the case. I'd love to teach Mr. Bearcat Meany how a real girl fights!"

"That," thought Encyclopedia, "is what Bugs wants."

He said nothing, however. When Sally was out to defend her sex, arguing was useless. He took a quarter from Ike's pocket and the three of them went to see Bugs. They found him sitting in the doorway of his clubhouse.

"Did you lose your way?" snarled Bugs.

"The ladies' sewing circle meets down the street."

"We've come to get Ike's two dollars," said Sally.

"You're a squirrel's idea of heaven," retorted Bugs. "I don't pay boys to fight like girls."

"Maybe you've forgotten how well a girl can fight," snapped Sally. "Shall I remind you?"

Bugs held up his hands playfully. "You know me. I'm too old to fight little girls," he said. "Say, wait a minute! You're in luck. There's a fifth-grader in the clubhouse. Maybe he'll box you."

"If I win, will you pay Ike his two dollars?" said Sally.

"Of course," said Bugs. "Am I not a man of my word?"

Bugs tossed a pair of boxing gloves at Encyclopedia's feet and disappeared into the clubhouse. His voice sounded from inside: "Some fresh dame thinks she can make you eat dirt, Bearcat."

Bearcat's little dark eyes studied Sally up and down.
"She don't look like much," he said slowly.

Encyclopedia picked up the gloves. Nervously, he pushed the right glove over Sally's hand and began lacing it. Ike did the same with the left glove.

Presently Bugs came out of the clubhouse. With him was a boy wearing boxing gloves. The boy looked like three fifth-graders: he was as tall as one and as wide as two.

"Bearcat," groaned Ike.

Bearcat's little dark eyes studied Sally up and down. "She don't look like much," he said slowly.

"She thinks girls can do anything boys can," said Bugs.

"I don't know," said Bearcat, tapping his knees without stooping. "I never boxed a girl before."

"She's been asking for it," said Bugs. "You know what? She said you'd have to fall down a well to get a deep thought. Would I lie to you? Give it to her!"

Bearcat shrugged. "If you say so, Cousin

Bugs," he muttered. He advanced on Sally.

Quickly Encyclopedia stepped between them.

"It won't work, Bugs," he said. "The fight is off. You made Ike hire us just so you could get revenge on Sally by putting her against Bearcat."

HOW DID ENCYCLOPEDIA KNOW?

(Turn to page 89 for the solution to The Case of the Knockout Artist.)

The Case of the Headless Runner

Riding the bus home from the Globe Theater, Encyclopedia wondered why he had done it. Why had he let Charlie Stewart talk him into seeing the triple-feature horror show?

He wished he had stayed home and read a book. He could have learned something useful.

Through the window of the bus he peered at the night sky. Clouds were gathering to the north.

"I'm going to be scared enough walking home in the dark without a rainstorm beating down," he thought nervously.

On the seat beside him, Charlie Stewart gave a shudder.

"I was fine through *The Headless Vampire* and *The Killer Gorilla*," said Charlie. "But those floating hands in *The Torture Chamber of Dr. LeFarge*—brrrrr!"

They were nearing their stop. Encyclopedia hoped some other passengers would get off with them.

"Pine Needle Lane," called the driver.

The two boys moved stiffly to the door. They were the only ones getting off. In a moment, they were standing alone in the dark night.

"It's spooky," moaned Charlie. "I know something terrible is going to happen."

"They were just movies," said Encyclopedia. "Nothing in them was real."

"Gorillas are real," insisted Charlie. "They can kill you."

"The nearest gorilla was in the Crandon Zoo, and he died last year," said Encyclopedia. "Now cut it out. There are no such things as headless vampires and hands that go around by themselves strangling people."

They began to walk.

"What about all the door lights that have been mysteriously broken in the neighborhood lately?" said Charlie. "Those floating hands—they always put the lights out before they attacked, remember?"

"Did you have to bring that up?" mumbled Encyclopedia.

The boys walked faster.

The night was growing darker. Storm clouds had blotted out the moonlight behind them.

They had to walk eight blocks on Pine Needle Lane and then four blocks on Rover Avenue to Encyclopedia's house. Charlie lived two blocks farther down Rover.

"Would you like to stay over at my house tonight?" Encyclopedia invited. "I'll use my sleeping bag."

"Thanks, but I'll make it home," said Charlie bravely. "Besides, there's not a light out."

It was true. Every house along Pine Needle Lane had a friendly door light burning. But the street and the spaces between the houses lay blanketed in shadows.

The boys had covered six blocks in record time when a bolt of lightning turned the night into bright day. As the lightning faded, a sharp tinkling noise sounded, followed by a mighty clap of thunder.

Charlie shot into the air as if he were practicing to be a human cannonball.

"D-did you hear that?" he whimpered. "It sounded like glass breaking." Suddenly he pointed and screeched, "*Yiiiiii!* I knew it!"

The door light in front of a house halfway down the block had gone out.

Encyclopedia stared at the blacked-out house. His eyes strained, searching the night-covered street for a pair of hands, or the ghost of the Crandon Zoo gorilla, or a headless vampire.

"Save yourself," squeaked Charlie. "I can't move."

"Try to run," urged Encyclopedia. "Try!"

"T-too late," chattered Charlie.

Something was hurrying toward them from the direction of the blacked-out house. As it drew closer, Encyclopedia made out a person —almost.

The person seemed to be waving his arms wildly above his head . . . only he had no head!

"P-please, feet," wailed Charlie. "Do your thing!"

His legs started going like sixty. Not running, knocking.

Encyclopedia was looking for a soft spot to collapse when the runner stopped and a head popped out. It belonged to Duke Kelly. Duke lived on the block and was one of Bugs Meany's Tigers. He had been pulling a shirt over his head while running.

Charlie gave a yowl of relief. "What are you doing out here?" he demanded.

"I was reading by the window," said Duke. "I must have dozed off. That clap of thunder woke me."

"So you ran down the street like a headless

The person seemed to be waving his arms wildly above his head . . . only he had no head!

vampire," said Charlie. "If I didn't have too much nerve, I'd have been scared sick."

"What's this vampire jazz?" said Duke. "I woke up and looked out the window. A bolt of lightning lit the street, and I saw two kids throwing rocks at Mr. Taft's door light. They broke it. I grabbed a shirt and tried to catch them."

"You chased them while putting on your shirt?" said Encyclopedia. "Most kids take off their shirts when they fight."

"Us Tigers fight like gentlemen," said Duke.

"You'll lose to a tree someday if you keep putting on your shirt while you run," warned Encyclopedia.

"Not this shirt," replied Duke, laughing. "It's a loose knit. I can see through it."

He tucked the shirt into his jeans and re-garded Encyclopedia and Charlie suspiciously.

"What are you two meatballs doing out at night?" he said. "Breaking door lights, maybe?"

"Good try, Duke," said Encyclopedia. "But

you have to do a lot better. You're afraid we saw you break the light."

HOW DID ENCYCLOPEDIA KNOW?

(Turn to page 90 for the solution to The Case of the Headless Runner.)

The Case of the Reward Money

Gus Elkin walked into the Brown Detective Agency. "I'm on my way to the city dump," he announced.

"Are you looking for something special?" asked Encyclopedia.

"I'm not going there to look," said Gus. "I'm going to listen to Wilford Wiggins. He's called a secret meeting at two o'clock. He promised to show us little kids how to make lots and lots of money."

Wilford Wiggins was a high-school dropout. He was so lazy he got dizzy spells thinking about getting out of bed in the morning. During the hurricane season, he opened his window and

40

waited for the wind to straighten up his room.

Most of his time was spent dreaming of ways to make money without working. Encyclopedia was kept busy protecting the children of the neighborhood from his crooked deals.

"What's Wilford selling now?" asked Encyclopedia.

"He wouldn't say," replied Gus. "It's something big, though. I've a hunch I ought to trust him."

"You're safer trusting an elephant to bring you a bag of peanuts," warned Encyclopedia.

"Maybe today will be different," said Gus.

"Wilford didn't tell me about the meeting," observed Encyclopedia thoughtfully.

"You've wrecked too many of his get-rich-quick schemes in the past," said Gus. "That's why I want you to come with me—in case Wilford's up to his old tricks. You know, smooth talk and a slap on the back."

"When Wilford slaps you on the back, he's trying to knock the money out of your pocket," said Encyclopedia. "Let's go."

"Okay, step closer. You've heard of the armored-truck
holdup in Detroit last week?"

The boys rode their bikes to the city dump. They arrived as a crowd of children was gathering around Wilford. He stood on an old wooden table, looking very aboveboard.

"I asked you out here because I don't want any snoopy grown-up stealing my secret," he began. "I know this place hurts the nose. But each and every one of you will walk home smelling like a rose after you hear what I have to say."

Bugs Meany shoved his way to the front.

"I didn't come here to smell anything except money," he said.

"Ah, the sweetest smell on earth," agreed Wilford with a grin. "Okay, step closer. You've heard of the armored-truck holdup in Detroit last week?"

The children shook their heads.

"You should read the newspapers," scolded Wilford. "A lone gunman got away with a million dollars in cash!"

"And you found the money in your lunch pail," sneered Bugs.

"Not likely," said Wilford. "But I know where it is."

"So tell us," shouted several children at once.

"I'm getting to it," said Wilford, holding up his hands for quiet.

"Yesterday," he said, "my pal Jim Baker took the bus from Glenn City to Idaville. As he sat down, the loudspeaker in the station blared. It said that the Detroit Armored Truck robber was believed to be in or around Idaville. Everyone was asked to watch out for a red-haired man who acts suspiciously."

"Let me guess," said Bugs, rolling his eyes in disgust. "Your pal Jim Baker spotted the robber on the bus."

"Well, it's true," Wilford said calmly. "As the bus started, a red-haired man in a brown suit spoke to a blond man sitting across the aisle. You know what he said?"

The children were silent as stones.

Wilford continued. "The red-haired man said, 'Did you hear the loudspeaker? I'd better slip off at the first stop. Get the money. It's in Detroit in my closet. But keep away from airports. Rent a car. Here's my address.' "

Wilford paused to let the suspense build before going on. "The red-haired man wrote on a piece of paper and gave it to his friend. Then he said, 'Memorize the address and tear up the paper.' "

Wilford held up a slip of paper. It had been torn into pieces and was taped together.

"This is the address where the stolen money is!" he cried. "My friend Jim picked up the pieces from the floor of the bus after the blond man got off."

Carefully Wilford returned the paper to his pocket.

"I have to beat the blond man to Detroit," he said. "I don't dare telephone the Detroit police. I have to see them in person to be sure of the big reward!"

"So you're putting the touch on us for the plane ticket?" asked Bugs. "How much?"

"The flight alone costs more than two hundred dollars," said Wilford. "I'm broke at the moment. So I'm letting all my young friends in on a sure thing. For every ten dollars you give me, I'll pay back a hundred!"

"Not so fast," grumbled Bugs. "How come nobody else on the bus heard the red-haired man talking?"

"Maybe there was too much noise," answered Wilford. "Or maybe he whispered. It doesn't matter. Jim didn't *hear* him. Jim has been deaf since birth. *He reads lips*."

"What's the robber doing around here if the money is in Detroit?" demanded Gus.

"The police have the serial numbers of some of the stolen bills," replied Wilford. "So he probably came east and spent some of the money here to make the cops think he was heading for Europe. Instead, he must have doubled back and gone west to Los Angeles. He's clever!"

"So is Wilford," Encyclopedia whispered to

Gus. "But not clever enough. Don't give him a cent!"

WHY NOT?

(Turn to page 91 for the solution to The Case of the Reward Money.)

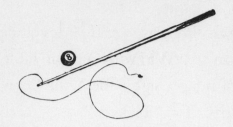

The Case of the Tooth Puller

"Who was that on the telephone?" asked Sally.

"Phineas Cole," answered Encyclopedia as he came back into the garage. "Phineas is pulling teeth at the First Church Summer Carnival. He wants us to come over right away."

"Did he yank a wrong tooth?" asked Sally worriedly.

"No," said Encyclopedia. "But he's afraid there may be trouble. He'll tell us about it at the carnival."

The two detectives closed the agency and biked to the church. The carnival was set up on the back lawn. Children and parents moved among the rows of tents and booths playing games of all kinds.

"There's Phineas," said Encyclopedia. He pointed to a booth with a pool table. Above the booth hung a sign: "Be Your Own Dentist. Win a Prize. Two Tickets."

"I'm glad you got here so fast," Phineas greeted the sleuths. "Something bad is going to happen."

He had to break off in order to see to business. A small girl had stepped uneasily to the pool table.

She eyed the shelf of prizes. Without a word, she handed Phineas two tickets and tapped her loose tooth.

"Don't be scared," Phineas said. "You won't feel a thing."

Quickly he tied a piece of string to the wobbly tooth. The other end he tied to the tip of the cue stick. He put a black ball in the center of the table and gave the girl a white ball and the cue stick.

"Make the white ball hit the black ball," he said. "Call your pocket. If you sink the black ball, you win a prize."

The girl lined up the white ball with the black ball. "Corner pocket," she said.

She gripped the cue stick tightly. Just before she shot, she lost her nerve and shut her eyes. The cue stick jerked forward. Out popped the tooth, but the white ball rolled wildly. It missed the black ball completely.

Phineas untied the tooth. He handed it to the girl, wrapped in paper. "Better luck next time," he said.

To Encyclopedia he added proudly, "I get a lot of repeat business."

"You didn't call us here to show us your do-it-yourself tooth puller," said Encyclopedia. "What's wrong?"

"Bugs Meany," answered Phineas. "Do you remember what he did at last year's carnival?"

Encyclopedia remembered. Bugs had stood near Phineas's booth and had sold pills for ten cents apiece. The pills were really only candy aspirin from a toy doctor's kit, but Bugs said they were pain-killers.

"Without pain to worry about, nearly every kid sank his shot," recalled Phineas. "I was cleaned out of prizes in three hours. Bugs was chased later, but he swore to get revenge on me this year."

"I don't see Bugs around," said Sally.

"You probably won't," said Phineas. "Bugs has an opening for a new Tiger. The word is out that he's giving some boy a trial today. If the boy does something to me without being caught, he becomes a Tiger. But nobody knows who the boy is."

"Has there been any trouble yet?" asked Sally.

"Plenty," said Phineas. "Take a look."

Coming between the rows of booths and tents was a parade of children in costumes.

"The parade is to build interest in the amateur show tonight," said Phineas. "The kids are

There were about thirty children in the parade.
Everyone had cuts and bruises.

marching to the auditorium for tryouts. Of course, some won't be good enough. Others will get stage fright when they see so many seats and head straight home."

"I'm not following you," said Encyclopedia.

"Look closer," said Phineas.

Encyclopedia looked closer. Ann and Willie Hallstrom, who sang duets, were limping. Ted Carter, who did hog calls, had his left arm in a sling.

Hank Ives, who did magic tricks, had a long scratch between his elbow and the bottom of his short sleeve. Kitty Bly, Idaville's best ballerina, had a bandaged arm.

There were about thirty children in the parade. Everyone had cuts and bruises. Many wore bandages.

"What hit them?" exclaimed Encyclopedia.

"A tent," said Phineas.

He explained. The performers had gathered in the office tent before the parade. Suddenly the center pole had mysteriously given way, and the tent had fallen. The children were treated by a nurse. Luckily, no one was seriously hurt.

"It's the work of the boy who wants to be a Tiger," said Sally. "I just know it is!"

"But how does knocking down a tent help Bugs get revenge on me?" said Phineas. "I saw the tent fall and ran over to help. When I returned to the booth, nothing was missing. I telephoned you just to be safe."

"Phineas!"

It was Mrs. Garcia, the carnival chairman.

"A roll of carnival tickets was stolen from the office tent when it fell," she said. "I just had a telephone call. The caller didn't give his name. But he said you stole the tickets and hid them in the pool table."

"That's not true," said Phineas. "See for yourself."

"I shall," said Mrs. Garcia sternly.

She dropped the white ball into three pockets. Each time the ball ran down the gutter under the table and came out in a shelf at the far end.

She tried a fourth pocket. The sound of the ball rolling stopped suddenly. She reached into the pocket and drew out the ball. She reached into the pocket again and pulled out what had blocked the ball—a roll of carnival tickets!

"Mrs. Garcia," said Encyclopedia. "Phineas didn't steal the tickets. But I think I know who did."

WHO WAS THE THIEF?

(Turn to page 92 for the solution to The Case of the Tooth Puller.)

The Case of the Girl Shortstop

Through the doorway of the Brown Detective Agency walked a girl with short blond hair and an angry face.

"Boys are rat-finks!" she said.

"Nonsense," objected Sally. "Some boys are very nice."

"Not if they play baseball," said the girl.

She tossed a quarter into the air, caught it behind her back, and slapped it on the gasoline can.

"I've come all the way from Glenn City to hire you," she said. "I want you to find out who learned I am a girl."

56

"Huh?" said Encyclopedia. Suddenly he wished he had gone fishing.

The girl explained. Her name was Edwina Silverstein, and she was nine. She lived in Glenn City. She had been the shortstop on an all-boy midget baseball team until last night.

"I joined up as Ed Silverstein," said Edwina. "My hair is shorter than most of the boys'. In a uniform and sunglasses, nobody could tell I was a girl."

"But somebody did," remarked Encyclopedia.

"One of my teammates followed me home after the game yesterday," said Edwina. "I saw him peeping through the kitchen window—after I'd put on a dress."

"And the dress put you off the team, but fast," said Sally.

"Two hours later Coach Pardee telephoned," said Edwina. "He said he was sorry, but I couldn't play. Girls are against the rules."

"How come you didn't recognize the peeper?" asked Encyclopedia.

"It was too dark," replied Edwina. "Besides, he had on his baseball uniform and sunglasses. All the players wear uniforms and sunglasses, and it's hard to tell them apart."

"Don't you even have a tiny clue?" pleaded Sally.

"Only this," said Edwina.

She took a pair of sunglasses from her pocket. "The boy tripped and fell near our fence when I chased him," she said. "The sunglasses went flying. He was in too much of a hurry to pick them up."

Encyclopedia examined the sunglasses. The piece of frame that hooked over the right ear was bent outward slightly.

"It must have got bent when the boy fell," said Sally.

"There are no marks or scratches," Encyclopedia pointed out. "So the frame was bent before he fell down."

"We ought to be at the next game Edwina's team plays," said Sally. "The boy without sunglasses is our man."

Encyclopedia shook his head. "You can buy these sunglasses in any drugstore. The guilty boy will have bought a new pair before the next game."

He returned the sunglasses to Edwina. "Still, it wouldn't hurt to watch a game," he added.

So the following Friday the two detectives rode the bus to Glenn City. Edwina met them at the station and took them to the ball field.

"I asked Coach Pardee what boy turned me in," she said. "He won't tell."

"Men are all the same," grumbled Sally. "They protect each other. They're afraid of what women can do if they get a chance!"

The children found seats in the stands as Edwina's team, the Bulldogs, finished batting in the first.

Sally pointed excitedly. "There's a boy without sunglasses!"

"He's the catcher," said Edwina. "He never wears sunglasses. He wears a face mask."

"Pooh!" said Sally in disappointment. "For a second it looked like an easy case."

The first batter up for the other team, the Hawks, drove the ball through the shortstop's legs.

"Tough one, Bob!" hollered Edwina.

She lowered her voice and said, "I feel sorry for Bob. He was the team captain and regular shortstop last year. But he was moved to left field when I beat him out. I guess he's a little rusty."

"He's jealous, that's what he is," snapped Sally. "Bob's our man, Encyclopedia. He spied on Edwina because he wanted his old position back."

Before Encyclopedia could reply, the next Hawk batter had knocked the ball for a home run.

"C'mon, Warren!" Edwina shouted at the pitcher. "You'll get 'em!"

Warren's lack of control for the rest of the inning was perfect. He never missed hitting a bat except when he hit an arm or a leg. Six runs were scored.

"*The Bulldogs should put in another pitcher,*"
Encyclopedia said.

"The Bulldogs should put in another pitcher," Encyclopedia said.

Edwina sighed. "After Warren, our pitchers get worse."

"The Bulldogs need worse pitchers like General Custer needed more Indians," said Sally.

"Don't be too hard on Warren," said Edwina. "He warmed the bench till our best two pitchers were hurt last week. Coach Pardee made him a pitcher because he's the only left-hander on the team."

She pointed to two boys sitting on the Bulldogs' bench. They were dressed in street clothes. One boy had his right arm in a sling. The other boy had his right foot in a cast. Both wore sunglasses.

"Dave broke his foot on the way home after pitching our last game," said Edwina. "Phil sprained his arm rolling out of bed the next morning."

"They could be lying," said Sally. "Either boy could have hurt himself falling by Edwina's fence. Gosh, Encyclopedia, I can't tell who's guilty."

"I can," replied the boy detective. "The guilty boy is—"

WHO?

(Turn to page 93 for the solution to The Case of the Girl Shortstop.)

The Case of the Rattlesnake's Rattle

Sunday afternoon, Encyclopedia and Sally went to the Museum of Science for the opening of the new children's exhibit, "Touch and Feel."

Small stuffed animals and fish, as well as shells and bones, were set on low tables. Mobs of little children were touching and feeling.

Encyclopedia was petting a rattlesnake when Chester Jenkins wobbled up.

"What time is it?" Chester asked.

"Half past two," said Encyclopedia. "Are you going someplace?"

"I'm staying right here," said Chester. "Cherry fruit punch and chocolate cake will be served at three o'clock. Cherry fruit punch is my favorite."

"I didn't know you had a favorite," mumbled Encyclopedia.

Chester was one of the nicest boys Encyclopedia knew. He was also the roundest. Once after lunch he fell down and rocked himself to sleep trying to get up.

"I've got half an hour to go," he moaned.

"You came just for the eats?" exclaimed Sally.

Chester sucked in his belly nine inches.

"I'm a volunteer guard," he said proudly. "I'm guarding the exhibit and helping the little kids. But I'll have to sneak off for a bite. I'm starving."

"You can't leave your post," protested Sally. "I'll bring you some cake and punch."

"Would you?" said Chester. Then he frowned. "There might not be anything left. This is a big crowd."

"Don't worry," said Sally. "My Aunt ·

Wanda is on the refreshments committee. I'll go early."

"Now you're talking," said Chester.

He moved away to watch the Touch and Feel Exhibit. Encyclopedia and Sally wandered into less crowded parts of the museum.

The two detectives lost track of time. It was five minutes before three o'clock when they remembered Chester. They hurried to the cafeteria.

Children were already lining up for refreshments. A long table was laid with bowls of punch, six chocolate cakes, and paper plates, cups, and forks.

Sally found her Aunt Wanda and explained about Chester.

"If he waits another minute, he'll bite anything that doesn't bite back," said Sally.

Aunt Wanda understood. She cut Chester the first piece of chocolate cake. It had seven layers.

"Chester could handle eight without even using his teeth," thought Encyclopedia.

Armed with the piece of cake and three cups

of cherry fruit punch, the detectives returned to Chester. He should have been delighted.

He wasn't.

"I lost my appetite," he said. "Look."

The tip of the rattlesnake's tail—the part with the rattle—was missing. Someone had stolen it.

"They ought to call this the 'Touch, Feel, and Take Exhibit,'" said Sally angrily.

"Did you see anything suspicious?" asked Encyclopedia.

"I was watching the cafeteria," Chester confessed miserably.

Suddenly he snapped his fingers.

"Hey, I remember something," he said. "Just as the ladies were bringing out the punch and chocolate cakes, Esmond Dinglehoofer asked me the time."

"What time was it?" inquired Encyclopedia.

"A quarter to three," said Chester. "Esmond said, 'I'd better get home or I'll miss the auto races on TV.' But he can't be the thief. The rattle was still on the snake when he headed for

"I lost my appetite," Chester said. *"Look."*

the front door."

"Esmond is in seventh grade," said Sally. "What was he doing at an exhibit for little children?"

"Let's find out," said Encyclopedia.

Esmond was on his front lawn when the two detectives biked up. He was making stink bombs.

"I thought you'd be watching the auto races on television," said Encyclopedia.

"Aw, I've seen faster action watching a zipper," said Esmond. "Nobody cracked up. So I came outside."

"You were at the Touch and Feel Exhibit at quarter to three," said Sally. "A little later the rattlesnake's rattle was discovered missing."

"So what?" snarled Esmond.

"We've come to get it," said Sally.

Esmond shook his fist. "What you see is what you'll get," he threatened.

Encyclopedia wished Sally didn't rush into things. "Someone stole the rattle while Chester Jenkins was looking away," he said quietly.

"Chester? That big tomato should have kept his eyes on the exhibit," said Esmond.

"He was watching the refreshments," said Encyclopedia.

"Listen," said Esmond. "The ladies were bringing out the punch bowls and the seven-layer cakes when Chester told me it was a quarter to three. I came straight home to watch television."

"So Chester told us," admitted Encyclopedia.

"But you're probably lying just the same," said Sally.

Esmond drew himself up to his full height.

"A lie has never passed my lips," he declared.

"Stop talking through your nose!" retorted Sally. She stamped her foot. "Ooooh . . . I wish I could prove you're guilty!"

"I can," said Encyclopedia.

HOW?

(Turn to page 94 for the solution to The Case of the Rattlesnake's Rattle.)

The Case of the World Traveler

A strange boy stepped into the Brown Detective Agency. He looked at Encyclopedia doubtfully.

"If you were to walk around the earth, how much farther would your head travel than your feet?" he demanded.

"That depends," replied Encyclopedia, "on how tall you are and where you walk."

"Say you're six feet tall, and you walk around the earth at the equator—twenty-five thousand miles," said the boy.

Encyclopedia did some pencilwork. "Your head would travel thirty-eight feet farther than your feet," he answered.

"Correct," said the boy. "I was told you had no leaks in your think-tank. Now I'm satisfied. You're my man."

He laid twenty-five cents on the gasoline can.

"My name is Hector Ames," he said. "I live on the west side, and I'm very interested in the earth. I want to hire you to listen."

"To the earth?" exclaimed Encyclopedia.

"No, to Justin Mudd," said Hector.

He explained. He was president of the Idaville Junior Ecology Club. Justin Mudd wanted to join.

"We always interview a boy before deciding whether to accept him as a member," said Hector.

"Why do you need me?" asked Encyclopedia.

"Justin claims he's been all over the world, even Africa. Our club could use someone like him. But we don't know enough to tell if he's lying or not. So I want you to listen to him."

"What makes you think he'll lie?"

"We go to lots of baseball games as a club," replied Hector. "Sometimes we don't pay to get in because we work hard for ecology projects in town. We get free passes."

"I see," said Encyclopedia. "You're afraid Justin is interested in saving money, not in saving land. I'll take the case."

The boys rode the crosstown bus to Hector's house. There, Encyclopedia was introduced to the club's officers. When Justin arrived, everyone took seats in the living room. The interview began.

Justin answered the questions put to him. Yes, he would collect old newspapers for recycling. Yes, he wanted to help stop pollution.

The questioning went on for several minutes. Justin handled himself well. Finally, Mary Dowling, the club's secretary, asked about his travels.

"We'd like to hear about the wildlife in other parts of the world," she said.

Hector leaned toward Encyclopedia. "This

is where Justin can help the club. We need an animal expert."

"I suppose I've seen just about every animal in the world," began Justin.

"Are they treated well in other countries?" asked Stan Fletcher.

"Usually, but not always," said Justin. "Once in Mexico I met a man who owned a fighting cock—an ugly, cross-eyed old rooster. I had my dad buy the rooster so I could retire it from fighting and find it a good home."

The children clapped in approval.

"Did you see any pigs in your travels?" asked Dona Frye.

"Dona has the largest piggy bank collection in Idaville," Hector whispered to Encyclopedia. "She's a pig nut."

"Once, flying over Germany, we passed over a pig farm," said Justin. "The pigs raised their heads to look at the plane and went running in all directions, scared stiff."

"Machines frighten animals," said Silvester

Braun angrily. "It's a shame."

"Have you seen any tigers?" asked Ken Wilson.

"Yes, when I was in Africa with my Uncle Ben," replied Justin. "We watched a tiger creep up on a family of giraffes."

"Oooh," whimpered Lucky Menken.

"All the giraffes ran away except one. It was lying on the ground, sick or something," went on Justin. "It tried to get up. But it had risen only on its front legs when the tiger killed it."

The children shuddered. It was a moment before the next question was asked.

"What was the strangest thing that ever happened to you?" said Molly Beal.

"In Australia, I went to a carnival and caught a thief," said Justin. "A man named Mr. Austin had a trained kangaroo, George. Mr. Austin picked pockets and used George to carry the stolen money to the next town."

"How did you catch this Mr. Austin?" asked Ted Wills.

"In Australia, I went to a carnival and caught a thief," said Justin.

"By luck," admitted Justin. "I happened to see Mr. Austin hide two wallets in George's pouch. Mr. Austin went to jail. George, his mate Frieda, and their baby Marmaduke were put in a nice zoo."

"Were you ever nearly killed by a wild animal?" asked Bill Cohen.

"You better believe it," said Justin. "My dad and I were camping out west. One night I noticed an owl in a nearby tree. That owl didn't move a muscle, but it followed our every move with its eyes. I thought it was going to steal some of our food."

"Did it?" asked Sam Benson.

"No, it saved our lives," said Justin. "We heard the noise of its wings as it flew away into the night, and my dad said, 'Something has frightened it.' He got his rifle—and shot a mountain lion prowling by our camp."

"Golly," Hector whispered to Encyclopedia. "Justin's had all kinds of animal experiences. Should we vote him into the club?"

"You'd be better off voting in a purple cow," said Encyclopedia.

WHAT WAS JUSTIN'S MISTAKE?

(Turn to page 95 for the solution to The Case of the World Traveler.)

The Case of the Lady Ghost

The Browns were sitting in the living room after dinner when Otto Beck burst into the house.

He was trembling like flypaper in a stiff breeze. His eyes bulged so far from his head he could almost stare himself in the ear.

He opened his mouth to speak, but he couldn't utter a word. His teeth were chattering louder than a tap dancer with spring fever.

"Otto, what is it?" exclaimed Mrs. Brown. "What's frightened you?"

"I—I saw *h-her!*" gasped Otto.

"Who?" asked Chief Brown.

Otto tried to tell. But the name stuck in a

fresh chattering of teeth. Instead he said, "I ran all the way from Heartbreak Cove."

"But that's seven miles," protested Encyclopedia. "Your feet must be killing you."

"My feet never touched the ground," said Otto.

He began sinking weakly to the floor. Encyclopedia shoved a chair under him.

"Thanks, I needed that," said Otto. After a while he recovered his strength. He blinked twice and said, "I saw Jennifer MacIntosh! She was dressed all in white, and the train of her gown dragged along the sand behind her. She was walking slowly, like a bride!"

Encyclopedia gave a start.

Jennifer MacIntosh had lived in Idaville a hundred years ago. Her lover had been lost at sea the night before their wedding. According to a local legend, Jennifer's ghost still walked Idaville's beaches in her long white bridal gown, searching for his body.

"Did anyone else see her?" asked Chief Brown.

"I—I saw h-her!" gasped Otto.

"I don't think so," groaned Otto.

He explained that he had gone camping on the beach alone. He had pitched his tent on the scrub grass above the sand.

"I was cooking supper when Jennifer MacIntosh appeared—"

He stopped short. His brow wrinkled.

Suddenly he said, "Hold on. There was someone else on the beach. About an hour before I saw Jennifer MacIntosh, a man walked across the beach carrying a bag. He seemed to be in a hurry. And he was limping."

"Limping . . ." muttered Chief Brown.

"Is that important, dear?" asked Mrs. Brown.

"Polk's Jewelry Shop was robbed after it closed today," said Chief Brown. "A witness says she saw a man leave the shop by the back door. She didn't pay much attention to him. But she remembers that he carried a bag and limped."

"Gosh, Dad," said Encyclopedia. "If the man really did limp, his footprints on the sand would show it. One step would be long and the other short."

"We'd better have a look," said Chief Brown. He got three flashlights and strapped on his gun.

As they drove to the beach at Heartbreak Cove, Encyclopedia questioned Otto about the ghost of Jennifer MacIntosh.

"Did you see her face?" he asked. "Did she make any noise?"

"I didn't hear a sound," replied Otto. "The ocean was making too much noise, and so was the wind. It whipped her bridal veil about her face. But I wasn't looking at her face. When you see a ghost, you don't look to see if she's anyone you know."

The questioning went on, but Encyclopedia could learn nothing more. Night had fallen when Chief Brown stopped the car on the south end of Heartbreak Cove.

He parked beside an old rotting dock. From there Jennifer MacIntosh's lover had put to sea, never to be seen again.

Otto shone his flashlight on his pup tent. It was pitched a good hundred yards from the water's edge.

"I was sitting by the tent when the limping man came by," he said. "Then an hour later I saw the ghost walk past from the opposite direction."

Three flashlights were used to search the beach for footprints. None were found but Otto's.

Suddenly Chief Brown halted. "Look here," he said.

Under the flashlight beams, Encyclopedia saw a trail of sand that had been smoothed over about two feet wide. It ran the length of the beach about fifteen feet above the high tide line.

"Someone has wiped away the footprints!" exclaimed Otto.

"Barney Slade and his wife live in a shack about two miles on the other side of the beach," said Chief Brown. "Barney has limped since he took a nasty fall last year."

"Is Barney the thief?" asked Otto.

"He might be," said Chief Brown. "I'd say Barney might have stolen a car and driven out here after the robbery. He probably then left the car by the old dock, hoping the police would believe the thief got away by boat."

"Instead he took a shortcut across the beach," said Otto. "He had his own car parked at the north end!"

"Yes," said Chief Brown. "But halfway across the beach, he noticed you. It was too late to do anything. He knew you were too far away to see his face, but he worried about his footprints. So after you ran to town, he returned and wiped them away."

"But there is no car except yours by the dock," said Otto. "And I don't think he'd dare chance smoothing out the sand. Somebody else might have seen him."

"Maybe he covered the footprints and then hid the getaway car," said Chief Brown. "Still, I agree. It doesn't add up."

"And I'm still stuck with the ghost of Jennifer MacIntosh," complained Otto. "No one will ever believe me!"

"Wrong," said Encyclopedia. "I believe you."

WHAT DID ENCYCLOPEDIA MEAN?

(*Turn to page 96 for the solution to The Case of the Lady Ghost.*)

Solution to *The Case of the Growling Dog*

Rover, an attack dog, was trained to hold strangers by the clothing.

But what if Rover had nothing to hold?

The poor dog could not do what he had been trained to do. So he would have a fit and break down.

That, Encyclopedia realized, is what had happened.

Ed had caught his shirt on the low branch, but not while he was crawling. The shirt was dangling from his hand!

For Ed was carrying his shirt—and all his clothing. He left his clothing outside the fenced yard.

Then he climbed the fence and walked past the confused Rover—*naked!*

Found out, Ed confessed to stealing Mr. Dale's tools.

And Rover recovered after a time.

Solution to *The Case of the Red Harmonica*

Bugs said he found the red harmonica on a trash pile at night.

He described the trash pile by Northcliff's house. He wanted Encyclopedia to believe that Northcliff had thrown the harmonica away or misplaced it.

But the only lights by the trash pile were blue.

So Bugs lied. He could not have seen something red shining in the blue light.

If only blue light shines on a red object, it would not appear red.

It would appear black!

Bugs gave back the harmonica—after he had dashed off a few bars of "Sad Heart of Mine."

Solution to *The Case of the Knockout Artist*

Bugs wanted to get even with Sally for licking him. So he tried to match her against his cousin, Bearcat.

He had Ike go to the detective agency with a fake story. Ike said Bugs owed him two dollars.

To get Sally angry enough to fight Bearcat, Ike claimed that Bearcat had said he fought no better than a girl.

But Ike got carried away with his role. He said he had hurt his hands on Bearcat's head. He couldn't even reach into his pocket and get a quarter.

Later, however, he helped lace up Sally's gloves.

He had forgotten his hands were supposed to be too sore!

But Encyclopedia hadn't.

Solution to *The Case of the Headless Runner*

From behind some bushes, Duke had thrown a rock at the door light—just as the lightning flashed.

The street lit up, and he saw Encyclopedia and Charlie approaching. He was afraid they might see him hiding or running back to his house.

So he made up a story. He had been awakened by the thunder. Then, in the flash of lightning, he had seen two boys break the door light. He had grabbed his shirt and given chase.

Impossible! Thunder comes *after*, not *before*, lightning. When the thunder roared, the lightning had already passed. Duke could have seen only darkness if the thunder had awakened him.

He was taking off his shirt as he ran toward Encyclopedia and Charlie, pretending to *be putting it on*, to make it look as if he had left his house in a hurry.

Thanks to Encyclopedia, Duke quit breaking lights in the neighborhood.

Solution to *The Case of the Reward Money*

Wilford read about the armored-truck holdup in the newspaper. So he decided to try for some easy money.

He made up a story:

The loudspeaker in the bus station told the people to be on the watch for the robber, a red-haired man. Then his friend Jim Baker spotted the man on the bus.

The story was good, but not good enough.

If Jim had not heard the loudspeaker, he could not have linked the red-haired man to the armored-truck robbery.

And Jim couldn't hear the loudspeaker.

Because Jim was deaf!

Thanks to Encyclopedia, Wilford did not get any money from the children.

Solution to *The Case of the Tooth Puller*

The real thief was Hank Ives, the magician.

He had pushed over the pole in the office tent. During the confusion, he stole a role of tickets.

When Phineas ran over to help, leaving his booth empty, Hank hid the tickets in the pool table.

Hank never meant to try out for the amateur show. He couldn't. So he made believe he had stage fright and left the auditorium before he was called upon to perform.

He might have got away with framing Phineas —but for Encyclopedia. The detective spotted him in the parade.

All magicians pull things out of their sleeves. So they must wear long sleeves.

But Hank wore short sleeves!

Solution to *The Case of the Girl Shortstop*

Warren, the pitcher.

The sunglasses that Edwina found were not scratched. Yet the ear piece on the right side was bent outward.

Thus Encyclopedia knew the wearer was left-handed. He had used his left hand to pull off the glasses, causing the right ear piece to become bent outward as it pushed against his head.

Had the wearer used his right hand, the left ear piece would have become bent outward.

So the boy who didn't want a girl on the team was a lefty. Warren was the only lefty on the team, remember?

When seen after the game, Warren had a bloody nose.

"He confessed," Edwina announced sweetly.

Solution to *The Case of the Rattlesnake's Rattle*

At a quarter to three, Esmond said to Chester, "I'd better get home . . ."

Encyclopedia knew Esmond had said that only to make Chester think he was leaving.

Esmond didn't go home. He went out of the museum and then slipped back and stole the rattlesnake's rattle.

Just before three o'clock, Aunt Wanda had cut Chester a piece of cake. The *first* piece.

Esmond was supposed to be home by then. Yet he knew the cake had seven layers!

He couldn't have known that unless he was in the museum and had seen Aunt Wanda cut the first slice.

Trapped by his own words, Esmond returned the rattle.

Solution to *The Case of the World Traveler*

Justin's mistake was in overlooking Encyclopedia, who spotted the following errors in his "true" adventures.

1. Roosters cannot be cross-eyed. Their eyes are on the opposite sides of their heads.

2. Pigs cannot look up at an airplane flying above them. Pigs cannot raise their heads.

3. There are no wild tigers in Africa. Tigers are Asian animals.

4. Giraffes, like cows and other cud-chewing animals, get up back legs first, not front legs first.

5. George, a male kangaroo, could not have a pouch. Only female kangaroos have pouches.

6. Owls' eyes are fixed and cannot move; also, because of their soft wings, owls make no noise while flying.

Solution to *The Case of the Lady Ghost*

Otto said that the ghost's long white gown had dragged over the sand behind her.

But it should have blown in the wind like her veil—unless it was weighted down. That was the clue!

Barney Slade had to wipe out his footprints in the sand. So he had gotten out his wife's old wedding dress and fixed her up to look like Jennifer MacIntosh. He had fixed a heavy board to the end of the dress's train.

As she walked along the beach, the board not only wiped away her own footprints, but Barney Slade's as well. When she reached the getaway car, she drove it to another hiding place.

Barney Slade was arrested and confessed. He had thought no one would believe what Otto had seen.

But he had not counted on Encyclopedia's quick brain to figure out his trick.